Little Rabbit Runaway

HARRY HORSE

PEACHTREE
ATLANTA

For Mandy

Published by
PEACHTREE PUBLISHERS
1700 Chattahoochee Avenue
Atlanta, Georgia 30318-2112
www.peachtree-online.com

ISBN 1-56145-343-9

Illustrations created in pen and ink and watercolor.
First published in Great Britain in 2005 by Penguin Books.

Printed in China
10 9 8 7 6 5 4 3 2 1
First Edition

Library of Congress Cataloging-in-Publication Data

One day, Little Rabbit was naughty.
Mama and Papa scolded him.

"It's not fair!" cried Little Rabbit.
"Everybody is always telling me what to do."

"I'm going to run away and live all by myself."

He packed a few things
for the journey.

"Don't go, Little Rabbit," said Mama.

"We'll miss you!"

"Good-bye," said Little Rabbit, and off he ran.

Little Rabbit ran far away.

Mama and Papa called after him.

He hid under a hedge.
"I'm going to build a house and stay there forever. I'm Little Rabbit Runaway. Nobody can tell me what to do!"

Little Rabbit had just started building
his house when along came Molly Mouse.
"What are you doing?" she said.

"I'm making my very own house,"
said Little Rabbit.
Molly Mouse asked if she could help.

Little Rabbit said she could, as long as
she didn't get in the way.

"We're going to need more things,"
said Little Rabbit, looking around.
Molly Mouse knew just where to find
everything they would need.

Little Rabbit and Molly Mouse carried back
as much as they could.

"I know!" said Little Rabbit.
"You can live with me."

So she did.
"Home, sweet home,"
said Molly Mouse.

The new house was very comfortable.
"I'll be Mama," said Molly Mouse as she set
the table and poured the tea.

They built the house together.

When they had finished,
Molly Mouse asked,
"Who's going to live
in this lovely house?"

"I am," said Little Rabbit. "It's mine! I'm Little Rabbit Runaway and nobody can tell me what to do!"

"I ran away too," said Molly Mouse.
"I don't have anywhere to live either."

"No, Little Rabbit," said Molly Mouse.
"Don't sit there. Sit here!
And sit up straight."

She made them a
special acorn cake.

She nibbled off a piece of cake
for Little Rabbit.
"Make sure you eat it all
up," said Molly Mouse.

Little Rabbit did not like Molly Mouse's cake.
"Yuck!" He spit it out. "I only like
my mama's carrot cake."

"What a naughty little rabbit you are," scolded Molly Mouse.
"No, I'm not!" said Little Rabbit. "You're not my mama
and it's not your house. You can't tell me what to do!"

He got up and bounded out the door.

"I'm Little Rabbit Runaway and I can do what I want to!" he said.
And so he did.

Little Rabbit rolled in the mud with the bullfrogs.

He jumped out and scared some ducklings.

"Boo!"

And he played in a thornbush
with a hedgehog.

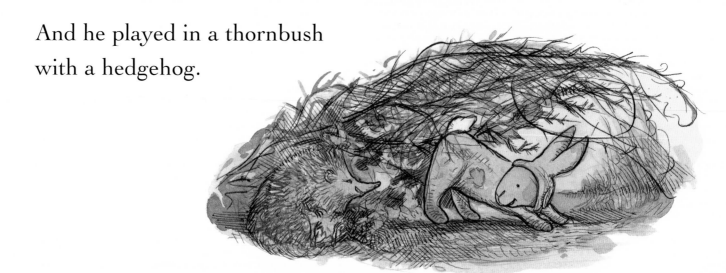

Soon Little Rabbit was very dirty indeed.
His blue suit was torn.

Then it started to rain.
Little Rabbit ran back to his new house.

"Quick, Molly Mouse. Let me in!" shouted Little Rabbit.

"Careful! You'll knock the whole house down," said Molly Mouse.

"I don't care!" he said. "It's my house! Let me in, you bossyboots!"

Molly Mouse let Little Rabbit
back in.
"Don't put your paws on
the furniture," she said.

Little Rabbit felt very sorry for himself.
"Never mind," said Molly Mouse. "I'll read
you a story to make you feel better."

Molly Mouse told Little Rabbit a story about a huge cat that chased after little rabbits who ran away from their mamas.

Little Rabbit got scared.

Molly Mouse got scared too.
She jumped into bed beside him.

"What's that noise?" whispered Molly Mouse.

"Is it the cat?" Little Rabbit whispered back.

Then came a thumping on the door.

BANG!

BANG!

BANG!

"It *is* the cat!" squeaked Molly Mouse.

"He's come to eat us up!" wailed Little Rabbit. "I'll never run away from Mama again."

The door opened . . .

"It's Mama!" cried Little Rabbit. He ran and hugged her.
"And my mommy too!" said Molly Mouse.

Little Rabbit had liked living in his own house, but he
was very happy to see Mama. He said good-bye to Molly Mouse
and then Mama took him home.

Later, after his bath . . .

and lots of hugs . . .

Little Rabbit told everyone all about his day
with Molly Mouse and his very own house.

When he was snuggled up in his real bed, Little Rabbit said, "I'm not Little Rabbit Runaway anymore, Mama. I'm just your Little Rabbit." Mama said that she was glad.

"Besides, one mama is enough for me," added Little Rabbit. "That Molly Mouse is a real bossyboots."